Festival in Valencia

by Anne Miranda

illustrated by
Robert Casilla

HOUGHTON MIFFL

Ana is visiting her cousin Rocío in Valencia, Spain.

It's time for the yearly festival called *Las Fallas* (**LAS FAH**-yahs).

3

Ana has been to many Mexican festivals at home in Texas.

Rocío says that *Las Fallas* will be very different!

A *falla* (**FAH**-yah) is a big statue. It's made of special paper called *papier-mâché* (**PAY**-per ma-**SHAY**).

Groups of people in Valencia often hire artists to make *fallas*.

5

Ana's family belongs to one of these groups.
Their *falla* is in pieces on this truck.

Everyone helps put up the *falla*. First, they
unload the pieces. Then they put the pieces
together.

All over
Valencia, people
are putting up
fallas.

Fallas often make people laugh. Many *fallas* poke fun at stories in the news. Some are made to look like famous people in Valencia.

Ana and her family go to see the *fallas*.
This huge one is in the main plaza.

The group has a party while the *fallas* are being judged. The best *fallas* will win prizes.

The next morning, Ana's family gets exciting news. Their group's *falla* has won a prize!

   Many people have special festival costumes. The
people in Ana's family have had their costumes
for many years. There's an extra one for Ana too.

This year, Rocío's mother has been chosen
to pick up the prize for the whole group.

Next comes a parade. People in the group love to show off their winning *falla*.

On the last night, Ana is in for a big surprise.
First, the fire fighters spray the buildings. This is so
the buildings won't burn. Then they set fire to the
fallas all over Valencia!

Everyone else is cheering, but Ana is shocked!
Rocío explains that the *fallas* are always
burned. It is the tradition.

Next year, their new *fallas* will be just
as wonderful!